THIS MONSTER ~~NEEDS SOME PATIENCE~~ CANNOT WAIT!

JUST READ
THE BOOK
ALREADY!

WORDS & PICTURES by:

bethany bARTon

DIAL BOOKS FOR YOUNG READERS   an imprint of Penguin Group (USA) Inc.

THIS BOOK IS DEDICATED TO:
MY TOTALLY AWESOME NIeces & NEPHEWS
SCHAEFER! JOEY! FRANKIE!
ISAAC! AVARI! ETHAN! EVELYN!

DIAL BOOKS FOR YOUNG READERS
A division of Penguin Young Readers Group • Published by The Penguin Group • Penguin Group (USA) Inc., 375 Hudson Street, New York, NY 10014, U.S.A.
Penguin Group (Canada), 90 Eglinton Avenue East, Suite 700, Toronto, Ontario, Canada M4P 2Y3 (a division of Pearson Penguin Canada Inc.) • Penguin Books Ltd, 80 Strand, London WC2R 0RL, England
Penguin Ireland, 25 St. Stephen's Green, Dublin 2, Ireland (a division of Penguin Books Ltd) • Penguin Group (Australia), 250 Camberwell Road, Camberwell, Victoria 3124, Australia (a division of Pearson Australia Group Pty Ltd)
Penguin Books India Pvt Ltd, 11 Community Centre, Panchsheel Park, New Delhi - 110 017, India • Penguin Group (NZ), 67 Apollo Drive, Rosedale, Auckland 0632, New Zealand (a division of Pearson New Zealand Ltd)
Penguin Books (South Africa) (Pty) Ltd, 24 Sturdee Avenue, Rosebank, Johannesburg 2196, South Africa • Penguin Books Ltd, Registered Offices: 80 Strand, London WC2R 0RL, England

Designed by Bethany Barton and Jennifer Kelly • Typography by Bethany Barton
Manufactured in China on acid-free paper

1 3 5 7 9 10 8 6 4 2

Library of Congress Cataloging-in-Publication Data
Barton, Bethany, date.
This monster cannot wait! / by Bethany Barton.   p. cm.
Summary: Stewart is so eager to go with his parents on his first camping trip ever that he will do anything to make the time pass more quickly.
ISBN 978-0-8037-3779-2 (hardcover) • [1. Patience—Fiction. 2. Monsters—Fiction. 3. Behavior—Fiction. 4. Humorous stories.] I. Title.
PZ7.B28465Thc 2013   [E]—dc23   2012017408

Special Markets ISBN 978-0-525-42705-6 NOT FOR RESALE
The artwork in this book was created using Higgins inks on paper & perfected in Photoshop.

VACATION IS ONLY A WEEK AWAY, AND STEWART'S PARENTS ARE TAKING HIM CAMPING FOR THE VERY FIRST TIME.

GET EXCITED!

TRAIL MAP

FLASHLIGHT

SLEEPING BAG

FIREWOOD

THERMOS

BACKPACK

MARSHMALLOWS

YUM PUFFS

IT'S GOING TO
BE SO MUCH FUN.
I ABSOLUTELY
CANNOT WAIT!!!....

BUT THAT'S JUST THE THING,
STEWART HAS TO WAIT.

FIVE. WHOLE. DAYS.

AWW MAN!
REALLY?!

HE EVEN BUILT A VERY
ADVANCED TIME MACHINE...

to the
FUTURE!!

BUT NOTHING SEEMED TO WORK.

STEWART'S MOM WANTED TO HELP.
LET'S BAKE COOKIES! SHE SUGGESTED,
IT'S A PERFECT EXAMPLE OF HOW
GOOD THINGS COME TO THOSE WHO WAIT.

I WANNA GO CAMPING

(AND THAT'S JUST WHAT HAPPENED.)

SO STEWART AGREED TO HELP
  PUT THE BOOK BACK TOGETHER...

AND TO DO HIS BEST
TO WAIT PATIENTLY.

SORRY,
FOLKS.

STEWART
WOULD LIKE
TO APOLOGIZE
FOR TRYING TO
RUSH TO THE END
OF THE BOOK.

APOLOGY
ACCEPTED,
KIDDO.

THAT'S FELIZ, STEWART'S BEST FRIEND.
SHE DOESN'T WANT VACATION TO COME.

NOT AT ALL!

WHAT?
HOW IS
THAT EVEN
POSSIBLE?

I'M GONNA MISS MY FRIENDS AND MY TEACHER, MS. RUMBLE, AND OUR CLASS PET, SNAPS, AND I JUST CAN'T LEAVE!"

WHAT A WEIRD REASON TO BE UPSET, STEWART THOUGHT.

ALL YOUR FRIENDS ARE RIGHT HERE!

AND MS. RUMBLE, TOO!

EVEN LITTLE SNAPS! →

YOU'RE SO WORRIED ABOUT NEXT WEEK
THAT YOU'RE MISSING RIGHT NOW!!

SOUNDS LIKE
SOMEBODY ELSE
I KNOW....

STEWART DECIDED TO TAKE HIS OWN ADVICE.

HE MADE THE MOST OF HIS LURKING LESSONS.

AND READ UP ON FOREST FRIGHTENING.